FASTER, SLOWER, HIGHER, LOWER

By Michael Berenstain

A GOLDEN BOOK • NEW YORK

Western Publishing Company, Inc., Racine, Wisconsin 53404

 Library of Congress Catalog Card Number: 90-85230 ISBN: 0-307-11570-4/ISBN: 0-307-61566-9 (lib. bdg.) MCMXCI

Faster,

slower,

higher,

lower.

Bigger,

smaller,

taller.

shorter,

Over,

under,

around

and through.

Up and down,

many, few.

Open,

shut,

out

and in.

Top,

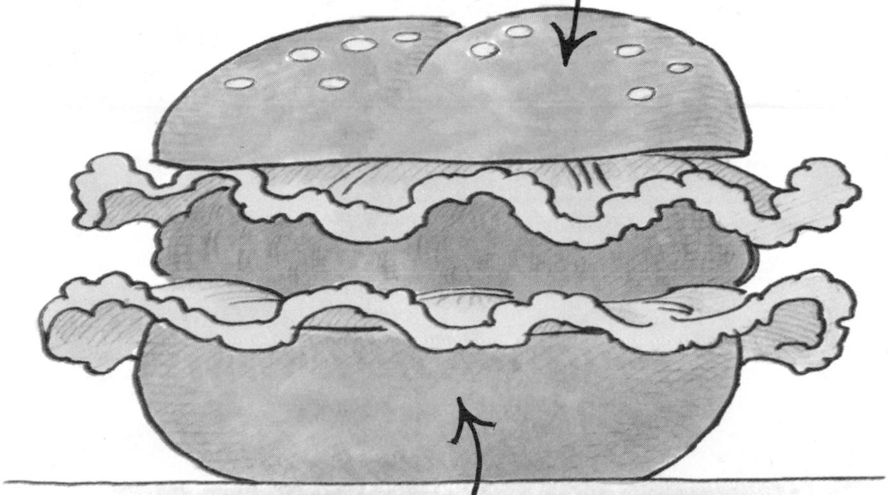

bottom,

thick

and thin.

LEFT
RIGHT
YES!
NO!

CROOKED
STRAIGHT
GO!
STOP!

Here, there,

short, long.

Hard, soft,

weak, strong.

ENTRANCE
EXIT
Hello!
Good-bye!
TICKETS

Floating,

sinking,

wet and dry.

Near,

far,

shallow,

deep.

Noisy,

quiet,

awake,

asleep.

Sick, healthy,

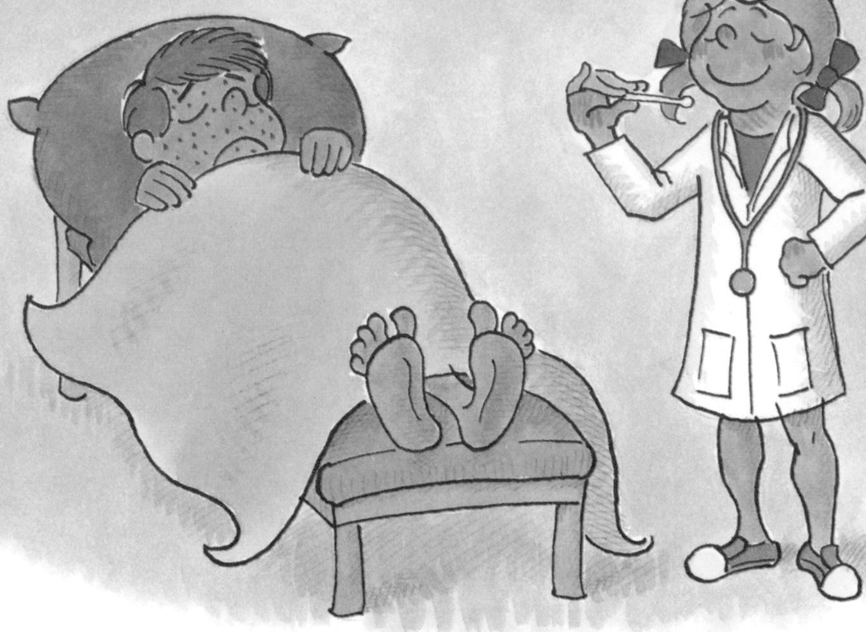

happy, sad.

Neat, messy,

good, bad.

On,

off,

dark,

light.

Wide,

narrow,

loose,

tight.

Warm,

cool,

hot,

cold.

Plain, fancy,

young, old.

Blunt,

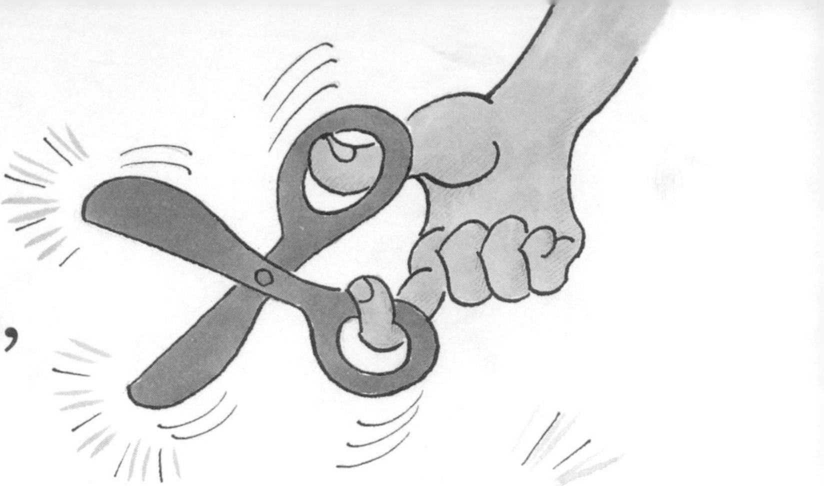

sharp,

smooth,

rough.

Sweet, sour,

tender, tough.

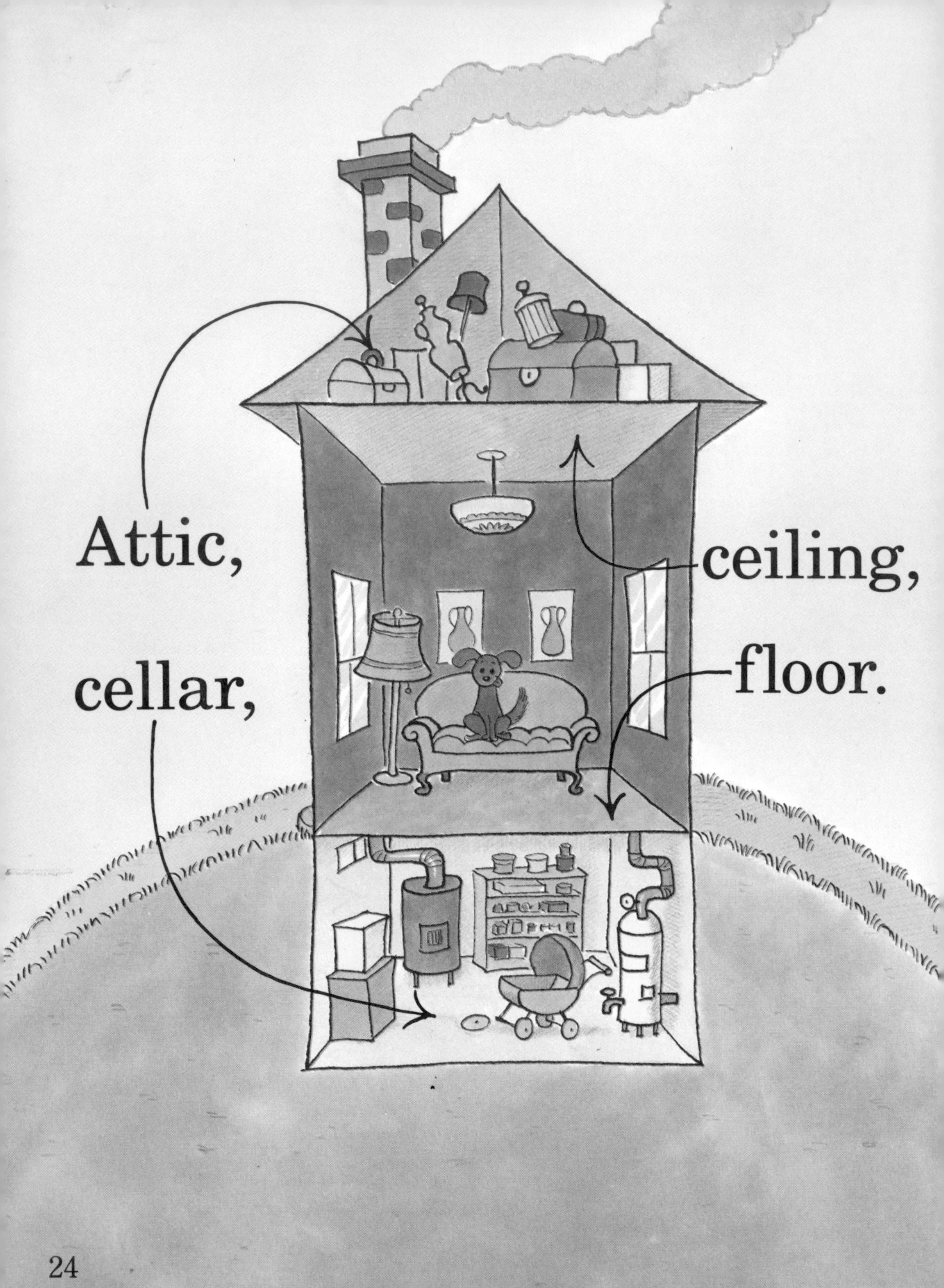

Attic, ceiling,

cellar, floor.

Huge

and

tiny,

less and more.

Forward,

backward,

flat,

bumpy.

Hero,

villain,

cheerful,

grumpy.

Apart, together,

push and pull.

Frozen,

melted,

empty,

full.

receive and send.

Early, late,

beginning . . .

end.